A Mom Named Dad

Kerri Lane

Illustrated by Edward Crosby

Rigby

Contents

CHAPTER ONE

An Impossible Project

"Quiet, please," said Mrs. Britain. The class finished putting away the art supplies. Then they went back to their seats. Everyone liked Mrs. Britain; she was the *best* teacher.

1

Lucy and her best friend Jane smiled at each other. Maybe Mrs. Britain was going to announce the "Best Citizen" awards. They'd both been working hard for the award and they could hardly wait to hear what Mrs. Britain had to say.

Then Mrs. Britain started talking, and Lucy's smile disappeared. In fact, with every word, Lucy's heart sank lower and lower.

"It's project time, class. And this time the subject is 'Mothers.' You have two weeks to complete your projects. And the good news is that we get to present them on Parents' Day. That means the whole school and all the parents get to have a look at our work! Isn't that exciting!"

A buzz went around the room. Some people were already making plans; others just groaned about more work.

Lucy still sat frozen. How could Mrs. Britain do this? She knew Lucy didn't have a mother! And after Parents' Day, *everyone* would know she didn't have a mother. Lucy's mother had died after Lucy was born, and Lucy didn't have a clue what mothers really did.

CHAPTER TWO

A Dad Who Juggles

As soon as the bell rang, Lucy raced out of the room. She didn't want to hear Jane bragging about her perfect mother. Or how she'd get the best grade for her project.

At the gate, Jane caught up to her. She was puffing from running so hard. "Why did you take off so fast? I had to race to catch up with you."

Then Jane said the words Lucy knew were coming. "Do you want to come over this afternoon and work on our projects?"

Lucy wanted to explode, but instead she told the truth. "I can't today, Jane. Dad and I are going to try a new muffin recipe."

❄ ❄ ❄ ❄

At home, Dad had all the cooking things spread across the kitchen table. Lucy's dad drew all sorts of funny drawings for advertisements, and he'd always worked at home so he could be with Lucy. He believed everyone should always be learning something new. This month it was juggling.

"How are you doing, Lucy Lu? Did you have a great day at school?" As Lucy's dad spoke, he was juggling three eggs.

Lucy sighed. Mothers would probably never juggle eggs.

"Dad, are you sure you're up to juggling eggs? You only started with oranges two days ago. And we had to squeeze all those for juice after they landed on the floor!"

"Sure I'm ready! See?"

Just then he missed and one egg came sailing toward Lucy. Her eyes opened wide. "Daaad! It'll break all over me!"

She put out her hands—half to catch it and half to try to protect herself from the splatter.

8

Suddenly the white oval shape plopped into her hand. Lucy shut her eyes tight and squealed. But nothing happened.

Dad's laughter rang out through the kitchen.

Lucy opened her eyes and glared at him. "It's hard-boiled!"

"Be gentle with it now, Lucy Lu!" Dad laughed again. "That's our lunch for tomorrow. Egg salad."

Lucy put the egg back into the refrigerator.

"Mothers would probably never throw tomorrow's lunch around the kitchen," she thought, as she washed her hands and started to mix the muffin batter.

Dad flopped an arm over her shoulder. "What's the matter, Lucy? You look sad."

"Nothing's the matter."

Dad picked up one of the mixing bowls, pretending to shove it over his head. "Oh, no!" he cried. "It's an attack of those horrible 'nothing problems' again. They're the worst ones!"

Lucy shook her head and read the recipe that was leaning up against the flour.

"Real mothers would probably never put mixing bowls on their heads," she thought. Lucy sighed again, and mixed the muffin batter some more.

While she did that, her father mashed the apples and added the cinnamon. Then he held out the muffin trays while Lucy filled them with the batter. "Are you sure you're okay, Lucy Lu?"

Finding a bright smile, Lucy looked at her dad and nodded.

Some Detective Work

That night, Lucy thought about her problem. She decided there was only one thing to do. She'd have to do some detective work. That would be the only way to find out what mothers really do.

The next morning, Dad was waiting in the kitchen. "Feeling better?" he asked.

She nodded.

"Good. Because I've got a great breakfast for you. Frog's legs on toast, covered in tomato and banana jelly."

Lucy giggled. "Yuck! Can't I just have the frog's legs on their own? I hate tomato and banana jelly!"

"What! You hate my jelly?" Dad exclaimed. "Just for that, you'll have to have cereal, juice, and a muffin!"

Lucy giggled again. Dad did this every morning. He was always thinking up silly breakfasts, but he always gave her something healthy. When she'd eaten, Dad asked, "Made your bed?" She nodded. "Good. Now, off to brush your teeth."

That afternoon, Lucy raced in and snatched an apple off the table. Then she gave Dad a quick kiss and took off to find out what mothers really do.

First stop was Jane's house. She could only find Jane's mom's feet, because the rest of her was under her old car.

"What are you doing, Mrs. Miller?"

"Oh, hi Lucy," came the muffled reply. "I'm trying to change the oil in my car." Then she laughed. "I just hope car oil is good for your skin, because mine is covered in it!"

Lucy frowned. Then she made a note in her note-book. "Mothers fix cars."

At Michael's house, his mother was painting a picture. And burning the spaghetti!

Lucy crept out. "Boy, am I glad I'm not eating dinner there tonight," she whispered to herself. On her notepad she wrote, "Mothers paint. Mothers cook." She looked at that last note and frowned. Then she added, "And sometimes burn dinner."

By the time she got home for her own dinner, her list was quite long.

She'd added:

Mothers tell you to keep quiet.
Mothers read books.
Mothers write books.
Mothers clean houses.
Mothers make you clean up your mess.
Mothers yell at you sometimes.

Mothers play golf.
Mothers work at all sorts of jobs.
Mothers dig holes.
Mothers plant gardens.
Mothers make clothes.
Mothers tell jokes.
Mothers work on cars.
Mothers mow lawns.
Mothers paint their nails.

Lucy scratched her head. It was all very confusing...

CHAPTER FOUR

What Mothers Do

For dinner, Lucy and Dad made a homemade pizza. They piled on lots of fresh vegetables and cheese, but she wasn't feeling very hungry.

"Is it still that 'nothing problem' that's bothering you?" Dad asked.

Lucy nodded.

"Want to talk about it?"

Lucy dropped her head. "I have to do a project."

"On what?" asked Dad.

Lucy crumbled the cheese fiercely. "Mothers."

"Aha," said Dad softly. "Now I see."

"I don't know what mothers do," Lucy whispered.

"Hmm. What about Bella?" asked Dad. "She's a mother."

Lucy punched him lightly on the arm. "Daaad! Bella's a dog! What can I write about her? That she rolls her kids around with her nose! That she teaches them to eat straight from a bowl and she picks fleas off their coats?"

Dad smiled. "Sure she does those things. But she also loves those puppies. She cares for them; she cleans them. She makes sure they eat and she keeps them warm at night, doesn't she?"

Lucy frowned. "I guess so."

"Then there's Katie, the cat next door. And even Peachie," added Dad.

Lucy rolled her eyes. "Daaad! Peachie is a parrot! She teaches her babies to fly! Real mothers don't do that!"

"If you're a bird mother, you do," he answered. "And don't forget Grandma, either."

"But Grandma rides her inline skates to the supermarket! And she's trying to get into the space program! She wants to fly to the moon! What kind of a mom wants to go to the moon?"

"My mom, I guess," he said quietly.

"Dad, what was it like having Grandma for a mom?"

Dad laughed. "She made me laugh. She loved me a lot."

Lucy gave him a kiss. "Just like you love me." She sighed. "But I still don't know what a mom really does."

In her room later, Lucy looked at her list. Then she thought about what Dad had said about the animals—and Grandma. None of it made much sense. How do you figure out what a mom does when they all do different things?

That's when it suddenly made sense. "I know what I'm going to do my project on!" she yelled.

Dad wandered in, wearing a silly brown thing with fake leaves stuck to it. It was about four times too small for him.

"Hey, that's great!" he said. Then turning in a circle, he asked, "How about this for the class play on Parents' Day?"

Lucy grinned. "Is that my tree costume?"

Her father frowned. "YOUR costume? Oh, I thought this could be what I wear."

Lucy laughed. "You're crazy, Dad. And yes, it's a great tree costume. Thank you."

CHAPTER FIVE

Lucky Lucy

On Parents' Day, all the projects were lined up around the walls. Lucy dragged her father over. "I didn't want you to see this until now. What do you think?"

Lucy had made a poster. The sides were covered in pictures and drawings. Some were of Bella and her pups. Some were of Peachie and her chicks. There was one of Grandma teaching Lucy to inline skate. (Grandma was the one wearing the space helmet.) There was one of Jane and her mom fixing the car. And one of Michael teaching his mom to cook.

In the middle, she'd written her idea of what a mother is.

"I want to read this to you, Dad..."

All mothers are different.
Some work away from home,
and some work at home,
Some cook, and some don't.
Some fix cars, and some don't.
Some skate, and some don't.
Some want to go the moon,
and some don't.
Some juggle and some don't.
Some are loud and some are quiet.
Sometimes moms have feathers.
Sometimes moms have fur.
And sometimes your MOTHER can
even be your DAD.
Because a mother is someone who
loves you and cares for you every day.
And so is a DAD.

At the bottom was a big picture of Lucy and her dad. Then Lucy turned to him. "You know, for a dad, you make a great mom!"

Dad grinned. "Thanks, Lucy Lu." Then he bent and whispered in her ear. "You know what I think we should learn this month?"

He didn't give Lucy a chance to speak before he rushed in with the answer. "Trapeze flying! Like they do in a circus!"

Lucy frowned for a moment. "Trapeze flying?" she repeated. "Would a real mother do that?" she wondered.

Then she laughed out loud. "Every mother is different..."

Lucy grabbed her dad's arm and gave it a hug. Lucy felt lucky—lucky to have a great mom named Dad!